Search for the Lost Jedi

**The galaxy is yours.
Be a part of**

**#1 Search for the Lost Jedi
#2 The Bartokk Assassins**

. . . and more to come!

EPISODE I
ADVENTURES

Search for the Lost Jedi

Ryder Windham

SCHOLASTIC INC.

New York Toronto London Auckland Sydney
Mexico City New Delhi Hong Kong

ISBN 0-439-10138-7

12 11 10 9 8 7 6 5 4 3 2   9/9 0 1 2 3 4/0

Printed in the U.S.A.
First Scholastic printing, September 1999

Search for the Lost Jedi

INTRODUCTION

In Galactic City on the planet Coruscant, the twelve member Jedi Council contemplated the Force and decided the action of over ten thousand Jedi Knights throughout the galaxy. Legendary for their bravery and power, the Jedi prevented wars, preserved peace, and maintained justice.

Jedi Master Qui-Gon Jinn was regarded as one of the greatest Jedi Knights. A brave warrior and a kind man, Qui-Gon was not intimidated by any challenge. He might have been a member of the Council but he believed his destiny was as a Jedi Knight, allied with the Force to help those in need.

As a Jedi Master, one must successfully train an apprentice — a Padawan Learner — to become a Jedi Knight. Qui-Gon Jinn's Padawan was a young man named Obi-Wan Kenobi. . . .

CHAPTER ONE

As the three armory droids lurched forward from the shadows of the arena, the twenty-five-year-old Jedi apprentice Obi-Wan Kenobi swiftly drew his lightsaber and pressed the activation switch. Suddenly, the sound of the lightsaber's low, steady hum filled the air, and the dark arena was illuminated by the weapon's cold, blue light. Despite his lightsaber's glowing blade, Obi-Wan could not see anything. He was wearing a thick, padded blindfold.

Snapping into a combat stance, the armory droids raised their blaster pistols. The droids aimed at the blindfolded Obi-Wan and fired, sending red energy bolts flying toward their target.

Using the Force to sense the trajectory of the oncoming bolts, Obi-Wan swiftly angled his lightsaber and swung at the deadly barrage. Loud, electrically charged crackling filled the air as Obi-Wan's darting lightsaber struck the energy bolts, batting them back at the three droids.

Two droids were destroyed as the bolts hit their torsos in a shower of sparks, knocking them to the black metal floor. The third droid was faster, jerking aside with surprising speed to avoid a direct hit. One energy bolt sped past it and smashed into the dense plastoid wall, but the final bolt shaved through the greased elbow joint of the droid's firing arm. Still gripping the blaster pistol, the severed arm clattered to the floor.

The droid reacted automatically. It used its remaining arm to reach for its back-mounted holster and pull free a fully loaded blaster rifle.

As the armory droid aimed the rifle, the blindfolded Obi-Wan Kenobi leaped across the arena, moving so fast that he became a blur. The droid recalibrated its targeting sensors, pulled the trigger, and unleashed an explosive stream of energy bolts at Obi-Wan's indistinct form.

But Obi-Wan was too fast — the spraying bolts hammered into the surrounding walls.

Instantly, Obi-Wan and his blazing lightsaber rematerialized close behind the armory droid. Detecting its opponent, the droid spun around to attack, but it wasn't fast enough. In a blinding flash, Obi-Wan's lightsaber slashed up through the droid, cleaving the automaton in half. It toppled over, its legs useless, its scorched, severed parts scattered across the black floor.

Obi-Wan Kenobi deactivated his lightsaber. The entire fight with the three droids had passed in just under eleven seconds.

"Most impressive, Obi-Wan," a deep voice commented from the entrance of the arena. Immediately recognizing the voice, Obi-Wan turned his blindfolded face to the speaker.

"Greetings, Master," the young Jedi answered as he removed his blindfold. "Forgive me. I didn't hear you come in."

Qui-Gon Jinn, a tall Jedi Master, smiled at his apprentice from the arched doorway. Moving his hand over a wall panel, Qui-Gon turned on the lights within the arena, causing Obi-Wan to blink his eyes. "You were focusing too much attention on the droids, Padawan," Qui-Gon observed. "To prepare for the unexpected, you must stretch out with the Force. Perhaps you're spending too much time here in the Jedi Temple. It would do you well to get outside of this training center once in a while."

"Yes, Master," Obi-Wan replied. "I'll follow your advice. But if I may ask, what brings you back to the Temple? I thought you were going to visit the lower levels of Coruscant."

"There was a change in plans," Qui-Gon answered.

"Sorry to hear that. I know how much you enjoy your friends down there." In truth, Obi-Wan did not understand why Qui-Gon liked the company of pathetic life-forms, such as those who populated Coruscant's lowest industrial regions. Over many centuries, the capital city had expanded until it covered the entire planet. The wealthiest citizens lived in luxurious skyscrapers while the very poor struggled for survival in the subterranean clusters far below Coruscant's surface. Changing the subject, Obi-Wan asked, "So, how much did you see of my practice session against the droids?"

Surveying the three fallen armory droids, Qui-Gon responded, "Enough to see your skill with a lightsaber is ever improving."

Grateful for Qui-Gon's praise, Obi-Wan bowed. "Thank you, Master."

As an eight-armed sanitation droid rolled into the arena to clean up the wreckage from the floor, Qui-Gon clapped Obi-Wan on the back. "Come along now, Padawan," he said, guiding his apprentice toward the exit. "We'll have to hurry if we're to attend the meeting."

"Meeting?" Obi-Wan asked, walking faster to keep up with the long strides of his Master. "What meeting?"

"We've been summoned by the Jedi Council," Qui-Gon replied as they left the training arena and entered a corridor. "That's why I was called away from the lower levels." The corridor was lined by a row of high windows, offering a spectacular view of Galactic City.

"The Jedi Council?" Obi-Wan repeated, clearly surprised. "Do you know why they want to see us?"

Leading Obi-Wan into a lift tube, Qui-Gon answered, "I only know that we'd better not be late!"

CHAPTER TWO

The Jedi Council was composed of twelve members: Mace Windu, Yoda, Ki-Adi-Mundi, Adi Gallia, Depa Billaba, Eeth Koth, Oppo Rancisis, Even Piell, Plo Koon, Saesee Tiin, Yaddle, and Yarael Poof. Together, they pondered the balance of the Force and helped guide the Jedi Knights in their missions. With Master Yoda at his side, Mace Windu presided as a senior Jedi of the Council.

Leaving the lift tube and entering the Council chamber, Qui-Gon and Obi-Wan passed Jedi Master Jorus C'baoth, who was on his way out. Since Jorus C'baoth was the personal advisor to Senator Palpatine of the Galactic Senate, Obi-Wan became even more curious about the nature of the Council meeting.

Approaching the members of the Council, Qui-Gon cast a quick glance at the seated Jedi. Immediately, he noticed an empty chair within the Council's semicircular arrangement. Realizing which Jedi was absent, Qui-Gon dismissed all formality and asked, "What's happened to Adi Gallia?"

Before Mace Windu could answer, Yoda's long, pointed ears bent back as he remarked, "Always perceptive Master Qui-Gon is, to what visible is not."

"Adi Gallia is missing, Qui-Gon," Mace Windu revealed. "She was on a covert mission to the planet Esseles." Raising a hand toward a holographic projector, Mace activated a hologram. A slowly rotating globe appeared, showing Esseles as a warm world covered with young mountain ranges. "We know Adi arrived safely on Esseles, but she missed the last two scheduled status reports. Are you familiar with this world?"

"I've never been there, but I know of it." Qui-Gon studied the hologram. "It's one of the planets linked by the Perlemian Trade Route in the Darpa Sector. Esseles' capital city is Calamar, a center for high-tech research and development, specializing in hypernautics and advanced hyperdrive engines."

Listening to his Master, Obi-Wan Kenobi felt both awe and respect. Obi-Wan had always been impressed by Qui-Gon's keen memory for details.

Mace Windu nodded, keeping his eyes fixed on Qui-Gon. "Esseles has progressed from research and development to full-scale manufacturing," Mace Windu noted. "Recently, the Council received a mysterious data card, alerting us that a factory named Trinkatta Starships was commissioned to build fifty experimental droid starfighters."

"Was the data card a trick to lure Jedi to Esseles?" Qui-Gon asked.

"If it were a trick," Mace Windu answered, "someone went to a lot of trouble to send us very detailed information." The hologram of Esseles vanished, replaced by a hologram of a sleek, dart-shaped droid starfighter. "According to the data

14

card," Mace continued, "these starfighters are equipped with hyperdrive engines."

"And know what this means we do!" Yoda interjected. "Travel through hyperspace for peaceful purposes, droid starfighters do not!"

"Master Yoda speaks the truth," Jedi Master Oppo Rancisis agreed. A cunning military strategist, the hair-covered Master Oppo pointed to the hologram and professed, "Droid starfighters have only two purposes: to kill and to conquer. They're flying hired guns without fear or remorse, generally reserved for the most lethal campaigns. With hyperdrive capability, they don't need to be transported by a carrier ship. Properly programmed, they could be sent to attack any ship or planet in the galaxy and bought by any creature with means."

"I doubt that Trinkatta Starships would have built expensive droid starfighters unless there was a ready buyer," Qui-Gon Jinn commented as the hologram vanished. "Do you know who commissioned these starfighters?"

"No," Mace Windu replied. "That's what Adi Gallia hoped to learn on Esseles. We haven't informed the Senate of our investigation because the droid starfighters may have been ordered by a member planet of the Galactic Republic. It's possible that one of our allies is plotting a civil war. If that's the case, informing the Senate might alert the buyers to cover their trail. We've asked Jorus C'baoth not to notify any Senators of these proceedings. Until we have solid evidence identifying who paid for the starfighters, we need to maintain secrecy."

"Secrecy?" Straining to keep his voice calm, Qui-Gon asked, "What of Adi Gallia? Is her life not worth more than yet another covert operation? In case you don't remember, I wouldn't be standing here now if she hadn't saved my life!"

Obi-Wan was surprised by his Master's statement. Qui-Gon had never told him of an adventure with Adi Gallia.

"This is why we have summoned *you,* Qui-Gon Jinn," Mace Windu answered. "You will lead two Jedi Knights to Esseles, to find Master Adi."

At that moment, two more Jedi Knights entered the Council room. They were Vel Ardox and Noro Zak. Wearing a black wet suit, Vel Ardox resembled a human, but she was an amphibious Blubreen from the Ploo Sector. Noro Zak's tapered ears and leathery, membranous wings indicated he was a Baxthrax.

Qui-Gon nodded at the two Jedi Knights. He had fought alongside Vel and Noro in the past, and trusted them both. "Except for the circumstances, it's good to see you," Qui-Gon greeted. Turning for the door, he continued, "The four of us had better get going to Esseles. Come, Obi-Wan —"

"Perhaps I was not clear, Qui-Gon," Mace Windu interrupted. "A Jedi Master is *missing*. This mission could be extremely dangerous. As an apprentice, Obi-Wan Kenobi is not ready for such an assignment. Your Padawan should remain here at the Temple."

Qui-Gon glanced at Obi-Wan, searching his face for any reaction. Obi-Wan wore a relaxed expression and wisely remained silent. But Qui-Gon sensed he was disappointed.

"Understood," Qui-Gon answered Mace Windu. "Obi-Wan will help us prepare for departure."

Watching Qui-Gon, Vel Ardox, Noro Zak, and Obi-Wan leave the Council chamber, Yoda said softly, "May the Force be with them."

In the starship hanger at the Jedi Temple, the Republic Cruiser *Radiant VII* and its crew of eight — a captain, two copilots, two communications officers, and three engineers — waited to transport the Jedi to Esseles. From the hangar deck, Obi-Wan watched as Qui-Gon followed Vel and Noro to the cruiser's main hatch.

Of course, Obi-Wan had hoped to join Qui-Gon on the mission. He had fought beside his Master before and believed he was well trained for such an assignment. But the Padawan knew better than to question Mace Windu's reasons for wanting him to stay on Coruscant. Also, he could feel relief within his disappointment. If Qui-Gon had argued with Mace Windu about allowing Obi-Wan to join the rescue team, it would have been embarrassing for the entire Council.

Entering the *Radiant VII,* Noro Zak had to duck, folding his thick-skinned wings tight against his back so they wouldn't scrape the ceiling. Qui-Gon watched from the open hatchway as Noro neatly arranged himself in a seat beside Vel Ardox. "You can close the hatch now, Master Qui-Gon," Vel noted. "We're all ready."

"Not quite," Qui-Gon replied as he fidgeted with the hatch mechanism. Turning from the hatchway, Qui-Gon looked to the hangar deck and called out to Obi-Wan. "Padawan! I want you to take a look at this hatch. I think it's stuck."

Wondering why Qui-Gon hadn't requested a proper droid mechanic, Obi-Wan left the deck and stepped into the cruiser. As soon as Obi-Wan was inside, Qui-Gon quickly sealed the hatch.

"Ah!" Qui-Gon exclaimed. "It seems the hatch works after all. Now, Padawan, since you're on board, you should find yourself a seat. We've a long trip ahead of us."

"B-B-But, Master . . ." Obi-Wan stammered. "Mace Windu said I should remain —"

"I know what Mace Windu *suggested,*" Qui-Gon

interrupted, "but you're *my* responsibility. If I'm going to Esseles, I want you where you belong: at my side!"

Obi-Wan's gaze traveled from the sealed hatch to Qui-Gon's face. Despite the presence of Vel and Noro, Obi-Wan was compelled to protest. "Forgive me, Master, but you put me in an unfair position. You ask me to disobey either you or the Jedi Council."

"I'm not asking you to disobey anyone, Padawan," Qui-Gon answered. "We both know you're ready for this mission. I want you to come to Esseles with us because I have a feeling we're going to need you there. If I'm asking for anything, it's your help." Turning to face the two seated Jedi Knights, Qui-Gon raised his eyebrows and asked, "Any questions?"

Vel and Noro swapped glances. Turning to Obi-Wan, Noro inquired, "Would you like a window seat?"

After a moment of hesitation, Obi-Wan stepped away from the sealed door. "I can't believe I'm doing this," he muttered.

Qui-Gon grinned. "Glad we sorted that out!" Leaning toward a wall-mounted comm unit, Qui-Gon addressed the *Radiant VII*'s captain, stationed in the cruiser's cockpit. "We're all aboard, Captain. Prepare to launch."

As Qui-Gon and Obi-Wan slipped into adjacent seats, Obi-Wan whispered, "Master? I was unaware that Master Adi ever saved your life."

Instead of answering immediately, Qui-Gon closed his eyes, preparing to enter a deep meditation. "I will tell you all about it, Padawan . . . *after* we rescue Adi Gallia."

CHAPTER THREE

Minutes after leaving Coruscant, the *Radiant VII* blasted into hyperspace. It was a difficult journey to the Darpa Sector, requiring the nav computer to delicately shift course from one trade route to another before reaching the Esseles system. Some time later, the cruiser exited hyperspace, arriving in orbit of Esseles.

"Trinkatta Starships is on the outskirts of the city, Calamar," Qui-Gon noted. "The captain will land our cruiser at a discreet distance and remain with the ship. From there, we'll deploy the landspeeder." Turning to the winged Noro Zak, Qui-Gon continued, "Noro, you'll fly to Trinkatta, scouting for signs of any unusual activity. Traveling by speeder, Vel, Obi-Wan, and I will meet you there."

Speaking into the cruiser's comm unit to the pilot, Qui-Gon Jinn commanded, "Take us down."

Twenty minutes later, Qui-Gon, Vel, and Obi-Wan's landspeeder zoomed away from the *Radiant VII*. Flying low over a dirt road, Vel Ardux guided the landspeeder at high speed toward the starship factory.

Trinkatta Starships was a huge complex, covering nearly two square kilometers. Surrounded by a high stone barricade, the complex contained two large structures: an observation tower, used to monitor incoming and outgoing starships, and a mammoth factory. The factory's upper levels appeared to be composed of plastoid with arched transparisteel windows, but the old foundation indicated the original building had undergone extensive renovation. Adorning the factory's roof, three tall chimneys pumped dark blue smoke into the sky.

Obi-Wan coughed, then cleared his throat. "That foul smoke," he gasped, nodding toward the chimneys. "I doubt Trinkatta Starships meets environmental regulations!"

Studying the high barricade that surrounded the factory, Vel Ardox noted, "It looks like they don't encourage visitors either."

Slowing the vehicle to a hovering stop near the wall, Vel Ardox gazed up, searching for Noro. Her sharp eyes quickly found the flying figure.

Noro glided high over the factory, carefully avoiding the rising toxic clouds that billowed from the three chimneys. Angling his wings, Noro swooped down in a spiraling descent toward the other Jedi. Seconds later, his taloned feet touched down on the ground beside the landspeeder.

"A long time ago, this factory must have been a fortress," Noro declared as Qui-Gon, Obi-Wan, and Vel climbed out of the landspeeder. Pointing to the observation tower, Noro continued, "Trinkatta's spaceport lies between that tower and the factory. I saw some repulsorlift vehicles and an old freighter parked in the spaceport, but there wasn't any sign of the droid starfighters."

"They might be within the factory," Qui-Gon mused. "Does the wall surround the entire factory?"

"Yes," Noro answered. "And on the other side of the wall there's a wide moat. A bridge crosses the moat from a security checkpoint."

"Show us the way to the checkpoint, Noro," Qui-Gon requested. Noro guided the others around the barricade to a large stone booth. Beyond the booth, a massive metal door separated the Jedi from the bridge to the starship factory.

Two tall security droids stepped out from the checkpoint booth. Approaching the Jedi, the droid's heavy metal feet clanked against the smooth stone walkway. One droid raised a hand, signaling a halt.

"What is your business with Trinkatta?" the droid asked as its barrel-shaped head scanned the four figures.

"We're looking for a friend of ours," Qui-Gon answered. "She was supposed to meet us here. She's a building inspector."

The droid shook its head, which creaked with each turn at the neck. "No building inspectors here. Only droids. You all must leave now. We're closing off the chimneys. The factory is about to be fumigated."

"Fumigated?" Qui-Gon asked. "But if there are only droids inside, what are you trying to exterminate?"

"Vermin," the other droid answered quickly. "Now you must leave . . ."

"Look!" Obi-Wan called out. Following his gaze, the other Jedi saw that the factory's three tall chimneys were no longer releasing toxic clouds into the air. Seconds later, the high transparisteel windows went dark as smoke began filling the factory.

Qui-Gon Jinn closed his eyes in meditation. Upon opening his eyes, he stated, "I sense Adi Gallia is within this complex . . . and she may be injured. We have to rescue her before she's consumed by the smoke!" Fixing his gaze on the droids, Qui-Gon commanded, "You must let us enter the factory *immediately.*"

The nearest security droid's photoreceptors turned red. "Instructions received from central droid control," the droid uttered as it took a step backward. "Trespassers must be terminated!"

Without further warning, both droids reached for their blaster pistols. Obi-Wan's hand darted for his lightsaber, but Vel Ardox moved faster. Her lightsaber blazed and lashed out in a sweeping flash, cutting down both droids before they could fire their blasters. The droids crashed to the ground.

"Security droids are supposed to *arrest* trespassers!" Vel exclaimed. "Someone reprogrammed these units to kill!"

"But who would — ?" Obi-Wan began but was interrupted by the bursting wail of a loud siren.

"The other droids must know we're here!" Noro stated. "One of us should stay here and distract them while the rest of us find a way into the factory. We have to stop that smoke or open those chimneys!"

"If we can reach the central droid control room," Vel Ardox added, "we should be able to override the system and deactivate all the droids!"

"Adi Gallia is our first priority!" Qui-Gon declared as he drew his lightsaber. "The factory is filling with toxic fumes! We have to find Adi and get her out *now!*"

At this point, you must decide whether to continue reading this adventure, or to play your own adventure in the *Search for the Lost Jedi* Game Book.

To play your own adventure, turn to the first page of the Game Book and follow the directions you find there.

To continue reading this Jedi adventure, turn the page!

QUI-GON JINN'S ADVENTURE:

SEARCH FOR THE LOST JEDI

CHAPTER FOUR

After quickly surveying the Trinkatta Starships checkpoint area, Qui-Gon Jinn turned to Obi-Wan Kenobi, Vel Ardox, and Noro Zak.

"Here's the plan," Qui-Gon Jinn told them. "I'll draw the security droids to the checkpoint and distract them while you three try to find another way into the factory. We'll have a better chance of finding Adi Gallia by splitting up and searching different areas of the complex."

"Shall we maintain communication?" Noro asked.

"If the factory droids are monitoring the frequencies, they might intercept our messages," Qui-Gon pointed out. "Use your comlink only if you need help or have located Adi Gallia. Go now. And may the Force be with you."

Obi-Wan and Vel ran off while Noro took to the air, leaving Qui-Gon alone at the checkpoint. Stepping over the fallen security droids, Qui-Gon approached the giant sliding door. He heard the sound of clicking gears as the door began to slide up into the high wall.

As the door rose, Qui-Gon could see the wide bridge that crossed the moat and led to the starship factory. Suddenly, six security droids emerged from the factory and lurched forward onto the bridge. Seeing Qui-Gon, the droids raised their blaster arms.

Moving faster than the droids' photoreceptors could follow, Qui-Gon activated his lightsaber and surged forward. Swinging the lethal blade with deadly accuracy, the Jedi Master cut down the six security droids within seconds. The droids crashed to the surface of the bridge with a clanging racket.

That should draw the attention of the other security droids, Qui-Gon thought to himself, hoping it would allow his friends to find another way into the starship factory.

Qui-Gon stepped over the metal bodies of the fallen droids, passing through the smoke that rose from their fried remains. As he began to cross toward the starship factory, Qui-Gon glanced below the bridge. Suspended ten meters over a deep, water-filled moat, the bridge was bracketed by low guardrails.

Switching on his comlink, Qui-Gon whispered, "I'm on the bridge that leads to the entrance. Are you inside the factory yet?"

"Not yet, Master!" Obi-Wan replied. "We ran into some more droids. Getting in will be more difficult than we realized."

Switching off his comlink, Qui-Gon was halfway across the bridge when a bright glint from above drew his attention.

Three stories up, on a rooftop that supported an elevated water tower, Qui-Gon caught sight of eight security droids running into position. Suddenly, the menacing droids raised their blaster rifles and fired from above.

Qui-Gon's lightsaber came up fast, striking at the oncoming energy bolts. He batted them back at the elevated water tower above the droids, striking the tower's base in rapid succession. As the droids continued firing, the water tower ruptured from the repeated battery and exploded over their heads, knocking them from the roof.

Thousands of liters of water plummeted in a devastating cascade, carrying the droids to the bridge below. Despite the fact he'd targeted the water tower, Qui-Gon Jinn was surprised by the magnitude of the resulting blast and turned off his lightsaber's power. In an effort to avoid being swept away by the torrential burst or crushed by the tumbling droids, Qui-Gon jumped over the guardrail and dived into the moat below.

After knifing into the water, Qui-Gon arched back to the surface for air. As he broke the surface, he was nearly struck by an energy bolt. Two droids had survived the fall to the bridge, and both were determined to kill the human invader.

Taking a quick deep breath, the Jedi Master dropped underwater and swam directly under the bridge, staying out of range of the droids' blaster fire. Swimming to the foundation of the starship factory, he saw what appeared to be the opening of an underwater tunnel. Qui-Gon hoped it might be an entrance to the factory. He reached for his utility belt and retrieved his breather. After placing the device over his face, he was soon breathing easily. He propelled himself forward into the dark tunnel.

Seconds later, Qui-Gon was engulfed by pitch-black darkness. The Jedi Master concentrated on the interior of the cave, using the Force to let him sense the rough, rocky walls. Absent of fear, he swam forward.

Soon, the tunnel narrowed, making it difficult to swim. Reaching out with his hands and feet, Qui-Gon could barely manage to crawl through the underwater access. He felt along the walls of the tunnel, trying to grab hold, but the stone walls were covered with an oily muck. He could not find a handhold.

Something slimy bumped against Qui-Gon's leg. In the next instant, his left ankle was caught in a tight grip.

Qui-Gon had company.

CHAPTER FIVE

Reaching to his lower leg, Qui-Gon touched a thick tentacle coiled around his foot. Snaking out from a hole in the tunnel wall, the tentacle tugged his ankle, drawing him into the gap. Some broken stones from the foundation lay below the hole.

Despite the creature's attack, Qui-Gon did not react with violence. It was in his nature to be empathetic to all life-forms. When he had been a Padawan, his tendency for kindness had often confounded his own Master. In the underwater tunnel, Qui-Gon found himself wondering, *If I lived quietly in a hole somewhere, how would I like it if some large organism came crashing through my home?*

Suddenly, the tentacle relaxed its grip and vanished into the gap in the tunnel wall. To Qui-Gon's amazement, he heard a soft, alien voice echo in his mind, responding to his own thoughts: *I apologize for attacking you, strange creature. I mistook you for a large fish. You are welcome to swim these waters, but be careful of the current.*

Behind his breather, Qui-Gon Jinn smiled. *Thank you.*

Leaving the creature behind, Qui-Gon swam on through the underwater tunnel. As he propelled himself through the darkness, his thoughts turned to Adi Gallia. Because she had rescued him some time ago, Qui-Gon believed he owed his life to her. But he also knew it was not the time to contemplate the past. The Jedi Master cleared his mind and swam faster.

A steady, mechanical thumping sound grew louder as he moved forward. He paused to listen to the sound, and realized that although he'd stopped swimming, he was still moving at a steady pace through the tunnel. Caught in a powerful current, he was being dragged deeper into the darkness.

Qui-Gon wished he had paid more attention to the tentacled creature's warning.

The mechanical thumping became increasingly louder. Battling the current, he extended his arms and legs, trying to brace himself within the tunnel. Unable to get a grip on the smooth, slick tunnel, he was dragged onward. In an explosive surge, Qui-Gon was launched out of the tunnel in a concentrated waterfall, spilling him into a wide, circular silo.

Tumbling through the air and falling water, he splashed down into a deep pool at the base of the silo. The thumping sound was nearly deafening, echoing off the silo walls in thunderous booms. Like a gigantic drain, the water churned and swirled around Qui-Gon, dragging him below the surface. Underwater, he realized the cause of the horrendous noise.

At the base of the silo, a giant hydraulic propeller spun rapidly, drawing the water down and circulating it in the factory's moat. Qui-Gon knew the great propeller would slice him to ribbons unless he could escape the silo.

Struggling against the downward flow, Qui-Gon broke the surface of the pool. Pounded by water falling from above, he swam for the silo wall. The inner silo appeared to be lined with thick layer of ferrocrete, a mixture of concrete and steel-like materials bonded at the molecular level. Like the tunnel, the slick walls allowed no purchase.

Looking up to the top of the silo, Qui-Gon saw a maintenance hatch. The hatch was illuminated by several greenish-yellow glow rods that dangled from a narrow beam. Qui-Gon considered throwing his compact grappling hook to the glow rods, but with both arms busy keeping him abovewater, he knew it would be a difficult effort. He also knew his breather's air supply was nearly exhausted.

Another possibility occurred to him. Saving his energy, Qui-Gon let himself be pulled beneath the surface. As he drew closer to the propeller, he concentrated on the spinning blades, visualizing them bending and twisting as they rotated. A loud cracking sound followed, then the propeller wobbled in its fixed setting. Using the Force, Qui-Gon had turned the machine's power against itself.

The result was an underwater explosion that shook the interior of the silo and shattered the propeller. Large bits of shredded metal sailed past Qui-Gon in a rush of bubbles as he broke for the surface. With the propeller's destruction, the steady thumping sound ended and the water level began to rise.

As the rising water carried him to the top of the silo, Qui-Gon quickly reached the hatch. Grabbing the wheel-shaped opening mechanism, he turned hard.

The rusted wheel crumbled in his hands as the water continued to rise.

He was trapped!

CHAPTER SIX

Qui-Gon tried concentrating on the hatch's unseen inner lock mechanism, but he found it difficult to remain calm. The rising water would soon be over his head.

The Jedi Master's hand reached for his lightsaber, tore it from his belt clip, and activated the blade. With a single, circular swing, he drove the lightsaber deep through the metal hatch. Then he deactivated the lightsaber and threw his weight hard against the center of the hatch, pushing it through its damaged frame. As the battered hatch crashed onto the floor of the next chamber, Qui-Gon leaped headfirst through the hole. A loud crunch sounded from his belt as he landed within a dry chamber. He had accidentally crushed his own comlink.

Qui-Gon quickly rose to his feet and lifted the hatch's wreckage. He jammed the cut metal back in the hole just as water began to spill into the chamber.

With the hatch sealed, Qui-Gon removed his breather and inspected his new surroundings. He stood in a large subterranean chamber. Dimly illuminated by glow rods, the stone-walled room smelled of dust and decay. In the center of the chamber, three tall pillars rose from the stone floor to the brick ceiling.

"Unnnnn," a voice moaned from behind one pillar. Running around the column, Qui-Gon found a semiconscious alien lying on the floor. A small yellow-scaled reptilian creature with a pronounced beak, the alien was clothed in a fine tunic. His left foot was chained to the pillar and his right arm was missing below the elbow joint.

"Are you okay?" Qui-Gon asked as he checked the alien's pulse. In this close proximity, Qui-Gon could tell that the alien's right arm had only recently been removed.

"Oh, I'm just fine," the alien groaned, "except that the droids cut off my arm and locked me up here to die."

Qui-Gon's eyes went wide. "The droids cut off your arm?!"

"They were trying to get information out of me," the alien said with a sigh. "No big deal. I'm a Kloodavian. The arm'll grow back in a couple of days."

"What are you doing in here?" Qui-Gon asked.

"I should be asking *you* that question!" the Kloodavian snarled. "I'm Boll Trinkatta! I *own* this starship factory! But my droids went berserk and took over. I don't know how, but someone must've reprogrammed them! The droids brought me down here and left me to die."

Before Qui-Gon could ask any more questions of Boll Trinkatta, an eight-armed maintenance droid rolled out from behind one of the other pillars. Hiding out of view, it had waited for the right moment to attack. Each of its eight arms wielded a different tool, including a beamdrill, fusioncutter, macrofuser, and power prybar. Extending its appendages, the droid accelerated on its treads and headed straight for the Jedi Master.

When the droid was nearly on top of its prey, Qui-Gon leaped aside. Unable to stop in time, the droid crashed into the stone wall. Falling back from the wall, the droid's eight arms flailed as it tried to recover its balance and get a position on the attacker. Before the droid could fire its fusioncutter, Qui-Gon's lightsaber blazed and arched through the air, slicing through the droid below its eight shoulder joints. The droid's head and shoulders tumbled from its body, sending a shower of sparks all the way up to the brick ceiling. Crashing to the floor, the droid lay motionless.

Stepping away from the remains of the fallen droid, Qui-Gon approached Trinkatta, who still leaned against the pillar. With surprise in his eyes, the Kloodavian remarked, "Only a Jedi moves that fast!"

"My name is Qui-Gon Jinn," the Jedi Master stated. Looking Trinkatta in the eyes, Qui-Gon came to the point. "A woman came here to inspect your building," he continued, maintaining secrecy by not mentioning Adi Gallia's name. "You will tell me where I can find her."

Trinkatta glared at Qui-Gon but did not answer.

"You're in a lot of trouble, friend," Qui-Gon continued. "I know you're selling fifty droid starfighters. I want to know the identity of the buyer. Direct me to your factory's central droid control room."

"I . . . I don't have to tell you anything!" Trinkatta insisted.

Qui-Gon was uncertain whether the Kloodavian was arrogant or afraid to answer his questions. Relying on the Force, Qui-Gon attempted to make the alien talk.

"You can tell me everything," Qui-Gon coaxed as he made a waving gesture with his hand.

Trinkatta's reptilian lips drew back into a good-natured smile. "Kloodavians are immune to Jedi mind tricks," he boasted. "But I'll answer your questions if you unchain me."

"Done," Qui-Gon agreed.

While the Jedi Master set to work on opening the lock, careful not to injure the Kloodavian's leg, Trinkatta spoke. "I don't know anything about a building inspector. It's possible she was captured by my droids after they'd already locked me up."

"What about the location of your central droid control room?" Qui-Gon asked.

"It's on Level 19 of the observation tower, on the other side of the factory's spaceport."

Working a thin wire into the manacle at Trinkatta's foot, Qui-Gon inquired, "And who ordered the fifty droid starfighters?"

Trinkatta gulped, nervous to answer this final

question. "I . . . I built them for the Trade Federation."

"The Trade Federation ordered these?" Qui-Gon said with surprise. "But this planet isn't anywhere near Trade Federation routes. Why did they commission *you* to build droid starfighters?"

"I don't know why they picked me," Trinkatta admitted. "Every starship maker in the galaxy knows the Xi Charrians have an exclusive contract to build droid starfighters for the Trade Federation. When the Neimoidians told me they wanted me to install hyperdrive engines into the fighters, I protested. The next day, my test pilot vanished! I was afraid if I didn't follow the Trade Federation's orders, they'd make me disappear, too."

"Where are the droid starfighters now?" Qui-Gon asked.

"I wish I knew!" Trinkatta squawked. "That's what my own malfunctioning droids kept asking me when they locked me up. Someone stole all fifty starfighters. When the Neimoidians find out, they'll kill me!"

"We'll worry about the Trade Federation later," Qui-Gon remarked as he removed the manacle from Trinkatta's leg. "Your droids closed off the factory's chimneys and the whole complex is filling up with fumes. If my friend is in the building, she'll die unless I can rescue her!"

"I'd offer to help," Trinkatta moaned, "but I'm

no good to you with this busted arm of mine." Aiming his beak toward a narrow hallway, he said, "That hall leads to the starship assembly room. You can open the chimneys from the assembly operations chamber. From there, you'll have to cross the spaceport to the observation tower and droid central control. I hope you find your friend."

"You can't stay here," Qui-Gon said calmly. "If the fumes reach you . . ."

"I can take care of myself!" the Kloodavian snapped back. "I have a secret tunnel that leads outside the factory. You'd better go while you can!"

CHAPTER SEVEN

Qui-Gon didn't want to leave Trinkatta behind, but the Kloodavian insisted. All his life, Qui-Gon had felt great empathy for all living creatures, especially for those who looked like they could use some help. Trinkatta may have been small, but Qui-Gon had no doubt that he was a strong-willed being, capable of taking care of himself. The fact that Trinkatta owned an entire starship factory was proof that he was a formidable character.

Qui-Gon ran down the hallway. The sound of his footsteps reached the audio sensors of two factory operations droids at the far end of the hall.

The two droids stepped forward, blocking Qui-Gon's entrance to the starship assembly room. Both droids had broad upper bodies supported on strong but narrow legs. Raising their arms, the menacing droids eagerly clicked their manipulatory claws at Qui-Gon.

Hoping to conserve the charge on his lightsaber, Qui-Gon's hand darted for his grappling hook. Tugging it from his belt, he played out the thin, strong wire and released the hook's claws. With a single whipping motion, Qui-Gon threw the hook at the droids' legs. The hook caught and circled the droids, snaring them below their knees. As the droids tried stepping out of the tangle, Qui-Gon pulled hard on the cable. The droids' feet flew out from under them, sending the two automatons smashing against the floor.

Qui-Gon leaped over the fallen droids as they clattered to the floor, unable to raise their bulky forms. He entered the starship assembly room and found it filled with a haze of smoke. Looking nine stories up to the ceiling, he could barely see the windows that lined the higher levels.

Across the room, beyond several rows of starships and repulsorlift vehicles at various stages of construction, Qui-Gon saw the assembly operations chamber. According to Trinkatta, the controls for the factory's chimneys were located in the operations chamber. Coughing, Qui-Gon checked his breather gauge. It was nearly depleted.

Holding his breath, Qui-Gon ran across the room. To his dismay, he found the operation chamber's computer circuits had been ripped apart. Qui-Gon suspected it was the droids' handiwork, an effort to prevent anyone from opening the chimneys and allowing the smoke to escape.

Qui-Gon spied an unfinished starfighter resting on a nearby conveyer system. The ship wasn't ready to fly but its laser cannons appeared to be operational.

Still holding his breath, Qui-Gon ran to the starfighter and leaped into the cockpit. His fingers flew over the vessel's weapon system as he aimed the laser cannons for the high ceiling.

Qui-Gon pulled the triggers and the cannons fired, launching a powerful blast of coherent lights at the ceiling. The laser bolts punched through the roof in a fiery explosion. The upper beams ruptured and fell. Qui-Gon leaped out of the starfighter and dove for cover into a grease pit. A split second later, the starfighter was crushed by a huge chunk of falling plastoid.

Looking up from the grease pit, Qui-Gon saw he had created a wide hole in the ceiling. His view of the Esseles sky was obscured by rising smoke as the fumes lifted through the hole and out of the factory.

As the smoke cleared, Qui-Gon scanned the area, looking for any sign of Adi Gallia. The Jedi Master sensed Adi had been in this room earlier. Not trusting his eyes, Qui-Gon closed them and opened his mind to the Force.

A picture formed in Qui-Gon's mind. He glimpsed Adi Gallia lying very still in a chamber. *She's nearby,* Qui-Gon suddenly knew. *Only . . . she's high above ground . . . somewhere . . .*

Turning his head, Qui-Gon opened his eyes to find he was looking through a window that offered a view of the factory's spaceport from the assembly room. At the far side of the spaceport, the observation tower loomed over the landing bay.

The tower! Qui-Gon suddenly knew he would find Adi Gallia there. Twenty stories tall, the tower was a new structure built on top of an ancient stone foundation. The first seventeen stories rose from the ground as a four-sided obelisk that supported an inverted dome — lined with transparisteel windows — that housed the three-story observation levels. Five plastoid landing decks jutted out from the inverted dome, adding to the tower's crude resemblance to a gigantic, machinelike flower.

Qui-Gon surveyed the tower and noticed a vehicle resting on the tower's uppermost landing deck. The vehicle hadn't been there when the Jedi had arrived at the factory. It was a bizarre two-seat skyhopper, a fast repulsorlift vehicle designed to fly above the ground. Qui-Gon didn't recognize the model.

Remembering that Trinkatta's central droid control room was on Level 19 of the tower, Qui-Gon thought the presence of an alien skyhopper seemed too great a coincidence. He suspected the parked skyhopper belonged to saboteurs, villains intent on taking over Trinkatta's factory by reprogramming his droids from the tower.

Realizing that Adi Gallia might be at the mercy of an unknown enemy, Qui-Gon ran for the exit to the spaceport.

He prayed he would find her alive.

CHAPTER EIGHT

There were several factory-owned repulsorlift vehicles parked on the tarmac. Hoping to reach Adi Gallia as soon as possible, Qui-Gon ran for the vehicles, planning to ride one to the observation tower.

As Qui-Gon approached, three late-model astromech droids rolled out from a transport that was up on blocks. Armed with beamdrills and welding tools, the battered old astromechs emitted a flurry of threatening beeps as they rolled toward Qui-Gon.

Brandishing his lightsaber, the Jedi Master ran around to the other side of the raised transport. The astromechs rotated their domed heads and turned back, hoping to corner the running man. As the astromechs moved under the transport, Qui-Gon slashed one of the supporting blocks. The transport teetered and the droids accelerated, trying to reach their target. Qui-Gon launched a well-placed kick to the side of the transport. The vehicle toppled off its blocks and crushed the rebellious droids.

Qui-Gon deactivated his lightsaber. As he raced to a parked landspeeder, he wondered whether Obi-Wan, Vel Ardox, and Noro Zak were still battling droids or if they had gained access to the factory. He jumped into a landspeeder, strapped himself in, gunned the engines, and raced for the observation tower. He would make every effort to reprogram the droids or shut them down.

As he neared the tower, Qui-Gon tapped the inertial dampers . . . but the landspeeder wouldn't slow down!

He pumped the inertial dampers again to no effect, then reached for the emergency lever. When the lever failed, he unbuckled his safety harness and leaped from the landspeeder. A split second after he hit the tarmac and rolled, he heard the speeder crash into the tower's foundation.

The Jedi Master rose from the tarmac and ran past the crashed speeder to the tower's lift tube. He entered the tube and stated his destination: "Level 19, droid central control."

The lift rose in a powerful rush from ground level. Seconds later, the repulsor field warning light flashed red and the lift screeched to a halt. Qui-Gon was launched off his feet, smashing into the ceiling's emergency escape hatch before he fell crashing back to the floor.

Rising from the floor, Qui-Gon checked the lift tube console. According to the numerical display, he was trapped between Levels 18 and 19, just shy of his destination. He realized the droids must have tapped into the lift tube computer terminal, and that his destination command alerted them to his exact position.

Reaching up, Qui-Gon opened the emergency escape hatch in the ceiling. Climbing through the hatch, he stepped onto the top of the lift.

Qui-Gon looked up into the cylindrical tube shaft and saw the sealed doors for Level 19. Suddenly, a whirring motor sounded from above. A shaft maintenance droid, clinging to the walls by its magnetic treads, rapidly descended from the upper levels of the lift tube. Aiming a disrupter at Qui-Gon, the droid prepared to fire.

Qui-Gon activated his lightsaber and threw it up into the air in a graceful spin. The lightsaber's blade sliced through the droid's left side, separating it from its treads and throwing it off balance.

As the lightsaber fell back to Qui-Gon, he caught it by the handle, then swiftly drove the blade through the doors to Level 19, carving a broad hole. Qui-Gon dove through the smoldering metal hole just as the rest of the dismembered droid came crashing down from above, slamming into the roof of the lift. The lift plunged down the tube, carrying the ruined droid all the way to the bottom. Rising to his feet, Qui-Gon heard the explosive impact as the lift struck the ground level, nineteen stories down. A fireball erupted, and Qui-Gon jumped out of the way.

Level 19 was filled with sophisticated computers but appeared to be devoid of any saboteurs or droids. Qui-Gon headed into the central droid control room and passed a window that offered a view of the starship factory at the other side of the spaceport. Across the tarmac, droids poured out of the factory and advanced toward the observation tower. There were over a hundred of them of various sizes, all brandishing weapons and lethal tools.

Every droid at Trinkatta Starships was coming after him.

In only a matter of minutes, they would reach Level 19.

Qui-Gon turned his attention to the interior of the control room. While searching for the main terminal that regulated all of the factory's droids, Qui-Gon stepped into a detention center.

The detention center was a long corridor that ended in a large black metal wall. Five cells lined the right wall and another five cells were built into the left. Instead of having sealed metal doors, each cell was viewable through a transparent energy field. From where Qui-Gon stood, he couldn't see directly inside any of the cells. He moved cautiously forward to inspect them.

Much to his amazement, he saw the same view in each cell: Adi Gallia's motionless body. Qui-Gon realized nine of the cells contained holographic projections, decoys to delay any rescue attempt.

In every cell, Master Adi appeared in the same position. She was slumped on a metal bed with her multi-tailed headdress spread out under her. Her eyes were closed. Her heavy brown robe prevented Qui-Gon from being able to see whether or not she was breathing. He yelled her name, trying to wake her. But it was no use.

A command console was located within the middle of the detention center. Qui-Gon eyed the ten unmarked switches on the command console, guessing that one of them should deactivate the cells' energy shields.

He cautiously selected a switch and threw it. Without realizing it, he had deactivated the holoprojectors built into each cell. Suddenly, all of the holograms vanished, and only the real Adi Gallia remained.

But the energy shield remained activated. There were nine switches left and Qui-Gon gave them a quick study. He suspected the switches next to the holoprojector switch might trigger a trap, so he reached for the fifth switch.

After throwing the switch, Qui-Gon heard a clicking sound from behind him. He spun to see a hidden door slide back fast from the black metal wall. A tall guard droid stepped out from a compartment within the wall. It was humanoid in design, but the droid's two arms ended in menacing, double-barreled blaster rifles. At the sight of the human intruder, the droid's photoreceptors glowed red.

The guard droid lurched forward. Qui-Gon's hand flew to his belt and his lightsaber was suddenly ablaze. The droid rapidly squeezed off a double burst of blaster fire from its arms, but the Jedi Master's blade struck each blast, hammering them back at the droid. The bolts pounded at the guard droid's armor and tore through its neck and joints. The droid's head exploded as its shattered body toppled to the floor, causing a crash that echoed through the detention center.

Qui-Gon deactivated his lightsaber and turned his attention back to the remaining switches. Normally, he enjoyed solving puzzles to keep his mind sharp. But with Adi Gallia's life at stake, he knew this wasn't any game.

Taking a chance, Qui-Gon threw both the seventh and eighth switch at the same time. He didn't know which switch had done the job, but all ten energy shields dropped.

He ran into Adi Gallia's cell, bent down, and checked her vital signs. She was unconscious and her pulse was weak.

But she was alive.

Barely alive.

Realizing she required medical attention, Qui-Gon moved fast to the main terminal of the control room. He hoped to transmit an overriding command signal to the droids, stopping them in their tracks before they could assault the tower.

After entering the commands into the computer, Qui-Gon ran to the window. Outside, the droids advanced closer to the tower.

Soon, they would arrive.

CHAPTER NINE

The saboteurs must have tampered with the computer. Qui-Gon wondered what to do next. Looking out the window, he could see the alien skyhopper was still parked on the outer deck that jutted out from the tower. Qui-Gon decided to make a run for the skyhopper, but not before he did something to stop the droids. Unless the droids were terminated, they might escape the factory and cause even more harm.

Turning back to the control room, Qui-Gon spied a red-and-yellow-striped emergency cabinet. Popping the cabinet open, Qui-Gon found it contained an auto-destruct initiator. Qui-Gon thought it was a dramatic bit of security for Trinkatta to have installed, but the device appeared to be the only way to destroy the droids. Wasting no time, Qui-Gon threw the initiator switch. The countdown began at three minutes.

Evacuation warnings sounded. Hopefully, the other Jedi would heed them.

Gathering Adi Gallia from the floor, Qui-Gon carried her up an access stairway to the tower's upper deck. Exiting the stairwell, he noticed the exit door had been kicked in from the outside. Proceeding through the damaged doorway, Qui-Gon wondered where the saboteurs had gone.

Reaching the upper deck, Qui-Gon Jinn carried Adi Gallia toward the parked skyhopper. Without warning, two tall insectoid aliens stepped out from behind the skyhopper. With their black body armor and segmented movements, Qui-Gon recognized the aliens at once.

They were Bartokks.

A race of bloodthirsty mercenaries, the Bartokks were notorious throughout the galaxy for their assassin squads. With their hive mind, they worked together to kill their assigned targets. Their intelligence was distributed through nerve centers throughout their bodies, so cutting off their heads would not stop them, since the severed pieces would continue to attack. Each Bartokk stood on two powerful legs and had four arms: two manipulatory arms extended from their waists while their upper arms ended in long hooked claws.

Before Qui-Gon could address the Bartokks, the two insectoid aliens raised their claws and stepped forward.

Quickly placing Adi Gallia on the floor of the deck, Qui-Gon drew his lightsaber and extended its blade. Like all Jedi, Qui-Gon did not believe in killing unless it was absolutely necessary. But he knew the Bartokks were professional killers who wouldn't hesitate to slice him from head to toe.

Seeing Qui-Gon's activated lightsaber, the Bartokks took a step back. The Jedi Master's eyes fixed on both of them as he warned, "This encounter doesn't have to end in your deaths."

The Bartokks exchanged a chittering communication, then sprang through the air.

Qui-Gon Jinn's lightsaber came up fast.

In a single sweep, Qui-Gon cut one Bartokk in half while relieving the other of an arm. The Bartokks screeched, and their severed parts clattered across the deck, reacting independently. Cutting down the upright Bartokk, Qui-Gon saw the insectoid body fragments scramble toward Adi Gallia's prone form.

Qui-Gon leaped to Adi Gallia's side. His boots landed on one of the Bartokks' writhing arms with an ugly squish. His lightsaber crackled as he brought it down again and again, hacking at the insectoid pieces. Qui-Gon knew he was running out of time. Since activating the auto-destruct mechanism, he knew he only had less than a minute to escape the tower. Switching off his lightsaber to lift Adi Gallia, Qui-Gon was nearly snagged by one of the Bartokks dismembered claws.

The Bartokks' body parts pursued Qui-Gon as he ran for the skyhopper. Placing Adi Gallia into the cockpit, Qui-Gon jumped in beside her and punched the controls. Although the skyhopper was designed for the Bartokks, it reacted to Qui-Gon's touch.

As the skyhopper lifted off the deck, a thunderous explosion erupted from below. The force of the blast pushed the skyhopper forward, nearly knocking the vehicle out of the sky. Gripping the controls, Qui-Gon banked hard to the left and came around to see fire and smoke streaming out from the top of the tower.

Glancing down to the spaceport below, Qui-Gon saw that the droids had all frozen — most were knocked down by the explosion. By destroying the central droid control room, Qui-Gon had prevented the droids from wreaking more havoc.

Landing the skyhopper outside the barricades surrounding Trinkatta Starships, Qui-Gon saw Obi-Wan Kenobi running from the factory's security checkpoint. Vel Ardox and Noro Zak were several steps behind him.

"Master Qui-Gon!" Obi-Wan called out as he approached the skyhopper. "We saw the tower explode! We couldn't even get into the factory. The droids held us back and . . ." Upon reaching the side of the skyhopper and seeing Adi Gallia's body, Obi-Wan was speechless. "You found Master Adi! Why didn't you tell us?"

"My comlink was damaged," Qui-Gon replied as he checked Adi Gallia.

"Good work, Qui-Gon," Noro congratulated.

"It's hardly time to celebrate!" Qui-Gon snapped. "Adi is unconscious and requires medical attention! Also, I couldn't find the fifty droid starfighters. But I learned they were ordered by the Trade Federation. Even worse, I had a run-in with Bartokk assassins."

Hearing this information, Vel, Noro, and Obi-Wan exchanged worried glances. If the Trade Federation and the Bartokks were operating Esseles, the Jedi knew their assignment had only just begun.

CHAPTER TEN

At this point, readers who chose to follow the adventure in the Star Wars Adventures Game Book can return to *Search for the Lost Jedi*.

"It appears Adi Gallia has experienced a massive shock to her system!" Vel Ardox exclaimed with great concern. "She must be taken to a medical center immediately."

"I'm afraid there's no place on Esseles that's prepared to heal a Jedi," Noro Zak grimaced.

"Wait!" Obi-Wan interjected. "There's a Jedi chapter house on the planet Rhinnal. Rhinnal is famous for its expertise in medicine and it's in the Darpa Sector. We can get Master Adi there in no time!"

Qui-Gon Jinn glanced at Obi-Wan Kenobi, then turned to Vel and Noro. "Carry Adi back to our cruiser and take her to Rhinnal," he told them. "Obi-Wan and I will remain here and investigate what's happening on Esseles, then meet you on Rhinnal as soon as we can. We have to learn what's become of the droid starfighters. If the Trade Federation and the Bartokks are involved, I'm determined to find out why!"

The Trade Federation battleship was far from home, positioned in space at the edge of the Colonies region. Standing on the command deck,

Trade Federation Viceroy Nute Gunray looked out a narrow porthole to see the Ringali Nebula. Gunray had followed his orders without question, maneuvering his battleship to the distant region where he waited for further instructions. After waiting seventeen standard hours, Gunray was becoming impatient.

Hearing a loud beeping from the communications console, Nute Gunray turned to his second in command, Rune Haako.

"We're receiving a transmission, sir," Rune Haako stated.

"Our instructions!" Nute Gunray exclaimed. "At last!"

A hologram materialized from the projector built into the communications console. A cloaked figure whose face was lost in shadow appeared before them. Nute Gunray recognized the projected image immediately.

It was Darth Sidious.

"Report the progress on the planet Esseles," the Sith Lord commanded.

"The droid starfighters were scheduled to leave the Trinkatta factory under the escort of a Corellian freighter," Nute Gunray replied. "The freighter should have arrived fifteen minutes ago. I cannot explain the delay."

Darth Sidious' hologram flickered. "Your report does not please me!" the Sith Lord hissed. "It has come to my attention that the Jedi Council has learned about the construction of droid starfighters on Esseles. Someone on Esseles must have informed the Council. Are you certain the starfighters will not be traced to the Trade Federation?"

"Yes, Lord Sidious," Nute Gunray answered. He was trying very hard not to sound nervous.

"Those starfighters are essential for our galactic expansion plan," Darth Sidious snarled. "Send someone to Esseles at once and confirm the droid starfighters have left the factory. Also, find the person who informed the Jedi Council and silence them . . . permanently!"

"Y-Yes, Lord Sidious," Gunray stammered nervously, but the hologram had already switched off. Turning to Rune Haako, Gunray commanded, "Prepare to leave for Esseles immediately!"

CHAPTER ELEVEN

On Esseles, Qui-Gon and Obi-Wan stood by their landspeeder with Trinkatta the Kloodavian. They watched the Republic cruiser lift off, carrying Noro Zak, Vel Ardox, and the wounded Adi Gallia up into the green sky. Seconds later, the cruiser vanished from view as it raced into space, bound for the planet Rhinnal.

Obi-Wan realized that Qui-Gon had yet to reveal the story of how Adi Gallia had saved his life. Looking at his Master's grim expression, Obi-Wan decided to wait for Qui-Gon to tell the tale.

"Thank you for rescuing me from my droids," Trinkatta muttered. Although his right arm was already starting to grow back, Trinkatta was still unnerved by the devastating events that had brought mayhem to his starship factory. His tunic was covered in dirt, a memento from the escape through his secret tunnel. Looking directly at Qui-Gon, Trinkatta said, "I only wish I could have prevented all this."

"I think Adi Gallia will be fine, Master," Obi-Wan commented.

"I *know* she'll be fine, Padawan," Qui-Gon replied with great confidence, "just as I know in my heart that the villains who wounded her will be brought to justice."

"Which villains?" Obi-Wan asked. "The factory droids, the Bartokks, or the Trade Federation?"

"I believe they're all connected," Qui-Gon mused,

stroking his beard. "Each bit of information is like a puzzle piece. The Trade Federation ordered fifty droid starfighters from Trinkatta's factory. When Trinkatta refused to install hyperdrive engines, his test pilot vanished, scaring Trinkatta into building the starfighters. Someone found out about the starfighters and was worried enough to send a data card to Coruscant, alerting the Jedi Council. Now it seems the starfighters have vanished as well."

"Don't forget the Bartokks," Obi-Wan added. "They broke into the central droid control room so they could reprogram Trinkatta's droids to take over the starship factory."

"But why?" Qui-Gon pondered. "What did the Bartokks want? The droid starfighters are no longer in the factory. Why would they — ?"

"If you'll excuse me," Trinkatta interrupted, "I've got travel plans. I'm getting off this planet before the Trade Federation comes looking for their starfighters!"

Suddenly, Qui-Gon Jinn's eyes went wide. "There's a good chance we might still be able to find the starfighters," he mused.

"How's that?" Trinkatta inquired, blinking his reptilian eyelids.

"The Bartokks travel in hives of fifteen," Qui-Gon noted, "but only *two* remained at the observation tower. The other thirteen Bartokks must still be on Esseles!"

"Why would they still be here if the starfighters are gone?" Obi-Wan asked, bewildered by his Master's logic.

"The starfighters are gone from Trinkatta's *factory*," Qui-Gon stressed, "but they haven't left Esseles!" Seizing Trinkatta by the shoulders, Qui-Gon lifted the Kloodavian and deposited him in the back of the landspeeder.

"We're not parting company yet, Trinkatta," the Jedi Master said solemnly. "You're going to help us find the droid starfighters."

NEXT ADVENTURE:
Fight the
BARTOKK ASSASSINS